Jake's The Name— Sixth Grade's The Game

by Deb Piper

Royal Fireworks Press
Unionville, New York
Toronto, Ontario

To John and Brett for their love and support!
Amanda, Willie, Kristian, Dan, and Jamie—
some very special people!
A Big THANK YOU to the staff, especially Mr. Kurz and
Mr. Ritter and to a very "unique" FIFTH and SIXTH
GRADE CLASS at Farmington and J.F.K. Elementary!
THANK YOU ALL!

Royal Fireworks Press
First Avenue
Unionville, NY 10988
(914) 726-4444
FAX: (914) 726-3824

Royal Fireworks Press
78 Biddeford Avenue
Downsview, Ontario
M3H 1K4 Canada
FAX: (416) 633-3010

ISBN: 0-88092-135-8

Printed in the United States of America on acid-free, recycled paper
using vegetable-based inks by the Royal Fireworks Printing Company
of Unionville, New York.

CHAPTER ONE

Jake Who?

Hi! My name's Jake! Jake Zulinski. Kind of a big name for someone who isn't even five feet tall but I make up for it with brains, wit, and of course, good looks. When a man's not blessed with an Arnold Schwarzenegger physique, you have to learn to use what's been given to you and fast, *especially* if you're in the sixth grade!

I'm not saying I haven't used my dynamic personality in the past, but sixth grade, from what I've been seeing, is a killer! I know it must be pretty bad because when I talk about going into sixth grade with my mom and dad, they kind of shudder as if someone put a whole tray of ice cubes down their backs. Their faces look real weird, too. They're all scrunched up! It's the look they normally give me when I tell them I have a report due tomorrow that's not finished and they find out I've known about the assignment for two months!

I've also noticed their lips developing an uncontrollable twitching motion they can't seem to stop. Especially my mom! She's been giving me these looks like I'm a bomb ready to go off any minute and she's been walking around mumbling a lot lately. At least I *think* she's mumbling. Her lips are moving and she seems to be saying something that looks like "my little baby!" My lip reading skills aren't the best but it makes me wonder if some diabolical disease is going to attack me now that I'm going into sixth grade.

Walking through my house, I've noticed mountains of magazines and books everywhere. I know my mom has always liked to read but she seems to be *glued* to whatever it is she's reading about now. It must not be very funny though, I haven't seen her laugh or even crack a smile in weeks!

Being the inquisitive person that I am, I decided to check out her mysterious behavior. I was really curious about what had my mom in this trance-like state!

I don't know. They all seem to be about the same thing. Something called *adolescence*. Whatever it is, it doesn't sound good!

Anyway, let's get back to some important information about an important person—me!

I'm probably never going to compete with Michael Jordan unless something drastic happens soon and my multi-vitamins trigger a super growth spurt, but I look on the bright side. I'll never hit my head on doorways or have a problem finding clothes that fit me.

My fire engine red hair has a mind and style all its own. I have freckles across the bridge of my nose that my mom says are signs of "character" and "a good sense of humor." Personally, I think it's a kind way of saying I look like Raggedy Ann's brother Andy with a strange personality to match! Mothers have to say nice things about their children, it's an unwritten law, kind of a "mother's code." It's all part of being a mom—I think.

Oh! There's one more thing maybe you should know about me. I'm deaf. People act kind of awkward and give you these funny looks for awhile, like you're not capable of riding the bus by yourself! I even had the boy who sat in front of me in science class last year ask my interpreter if she had to go home with me at night. Can you believe it?

Unfortunately, all too quickly, everyone usually catches on that I can be just as mischievous or angelic as everyone else. Sometimes it makes a difference, but mostly I'm just like everyone else. I just can't hear.

CHAPTER TWO

The Power Zone

The first day of school as I stroll down the familiar hallways of Li:.coln Elementary School like I have since kindergarten, this sudden tingling starts in my toes and works its way up my body. What is it I wonder? What's happening?

I continue past the kindergarten rooms, carefully avoiding the latest in high tech cameras and video equipment recording "The First Day Of School." Another in a series of tapes for the "home video" collection of most embarrassing moments you would rather forget but your parents think are precious and adorable.

With my lightning quick reflexes, I expertly dodge several crying children attached to their mothers' legs like extra large pieces of Velcro!

I weave my way down the hallway of first, second, and third graders. Past the newest line of Beauty and the Beast, Barney, and Big Bird lunch boxes, backpacks, and Trapperkeepers.

I turn the corner past the fourth and fifth graders. The boys are busy pushing each other around, unable to keep their hands to themselves. The girls are grouped together eyeing the boys like they're rejected aliens from another planet.

As I continue my journey, this strange feeling seems to be growing even stronger. I can feel myself becoming taller with each step I take. My usual, "I'd rather be anywhere but here" walk seems to be transforming into a "cool" strut! I don't understand! What's happening to me?

I look up. Shafts of bright sunlight bounce off particles of dust, like diamonds, creating a hazy, swirling fog. Wow!

Is this a dream? Maybe I've been transported to another time dimension? "Beam me up, Scottie!"

I slowly look up and I see—it—in all its splendor! It's everything I thought—it—would be...

The Sixth Grade Hallway!

Suddenly I realize what this means. We are the oldest! The top of the heap! There are no big "thugs" to boss us around, tease us, or just plain give us a hard time. No sireeee! Those "thugs" are us! I can't believe it! Our day has finally come! *We* have the ultimate power!

Out of nowhere a chill races down my spine as a giant shadow looms across my path casting a huge dark cloud from the doorway. What is it? What evil force is lurking in the shadows to dampen such a glorious day? What could it possibly be?

"The Teacher."

CHAPTER THREE

The First Day Blues

No matter what grade you're in, the first day of school is the worst! Everyone looks at you like they've never seen you before or you've grown two heads over the summer.

The kids act strange and it seems this year, even stranger! I can't put my finger on it yet but I'll figure it out if it takes me all year. After all, I am a rather brilliant human being!

There is one thing that will never change on the first day of school. It's "the speech." You know the one! It's the lecture teachers never seem to tire of. "The rules and consequences." Actually, they seem to enjoy it!

I would like to pause here for a moment and give you one example of the *benefits* of being deaf. "Benefits?" you say? You better believe it! Once my interpreter signs the "rules and consequences" the first time, I pretty much know what's going on. So, when she starts signing "the rules" for each teacher as the day goes on, I find better things to do!

Top priority today is looking longingly out the window at the beautiful, sunny, late summer's day I'm missing,. thinking of all the fun I could be having!

They start school entirely too early! October would be better, but fall can be awfully nice. Well, November's OK, but you wouldn't want to interfere with Thanksgiving. We could wait until December and have two weeks Christmas vacation! We could break in nice and slow! That sounds good. But there *is* skiing, sledding, skating...!

Daydreaming can be great but it has its consequences too if I get caught. My interpreter tends to get a *teensy* bit grumpy when I "tune out." Actually, there are days when I could start a forest fire from the sparks flying from her eyes and I know I'm in for a "tuning in" and "tuning out" lecture!

5

Anyway, back to the "first day blues." Here I am, feeling all this power and the teacher starts giving us another lecture. "Now that you're sixth graders, we will expect more from you. It's time to start acting like young adults! Sixth grade is an important stepping stone in preparing yourselves for the BIG step! Junior high school!"

Junior high school! Hold on a second! That's PRESSURE with a capital "P." This is only the first day of sixth grade! Can't we savor our power for awhile?

I like being young and immature! Who wants maturity and responsibility? Who wants to be a *sevy* anyway! I want to have fun! I've waited six long years for this moment. I want to enjoy each and every one of them!

Boy! Just when you think you've got it made, you find out there's a catch. Gee! And I thought sixth grade was going to be so great!

CHAPTER FOUR

The Difference

The first day of school is a little more hectic for me because I have to meet with my interpreter and get my auditory trainer and microphone for class.

In case you've never heard of an auditory trainer, it's a small box I clip on to my belt with a big soft rubber loop attached that goes around my neck. The teacher wears a microphone that looks like a "fat tie" looped around his or her neck.

This equipment is supposed to help me know when the teacher is talking. I don't really like it but it's better than the old trainers I had when I was little. The teacher would strap this big box on my chest with a harness that made me look like a horse or a dog! The trainer I have now, I can put under my shirt, and you don't notice it at all.

The interpreters you notice a lot more. They're hard to hide! I've been lucky. My interpreters have all been nice and my classmates are so used to having an interpreter in the classroom with the regular teacher, it seems normal to them.

To be honest, sometimes it's more fun to watch the interpreter than the teacher—especially when you're bored!

Oh! I guess I should explain what an interpreter is, just in case you don't know. An interpreter is a person who goes with me to my classes all day to use sign language to communicate what the teacher is saying. Most of the time we become good friends but you have to remember they can become just as angry as the teacher if you try and pull something on them. What's important to remember is, they're not nearly as easy to fool as the teachers!

Take for example, my interpreter, Mrs. Berge. She shoots off like the space shuttle when I say, "I don't understand? Do you think you could *give* me the answer?" Of course at the same time I hit her full power with my "not a friend in the world" look.

You know the look! It's the one you give your mom and dad when you're pretty sure they're going to say "no." You start with big sad eyes, hunch your shoulders slightly forward like there's a ton of bricks on them, then add a heavy sigh! That's always good! To perfect "the look" and really grab their heartstrings, make your bottom lip stick out and quiver, just a little! Not too much! You don't want to overdo it. You have to look sincere. That will get them every time!

Unfortunately, my interpreter caught on to my act right away. Drats! Mrs. Berge has been my interpreter for two years, and she knows me too well. I thought I had perfected it so well, I was saving a place in my trophy case for an Academy Award. I was ready to start teaching my craft to younger classmates for a nominal fee, of course. You just don't give away secrets you've worked years to perfect!

Mrs. Berge did not feel the same and suggested I channel my expertise in acting to something more suitable, the yearly class program maybe? In her words, "It would be a shame to waste such creative talent." I'm still trying to figure out if that was a compliment? Oh well!

The beginning of the school year can be a little awkward for the teachers who have never had a deaf student in their classroom before.

First of all, the teachers have to get used to wearing the microphone they put around their necks. Some teachers look at the microphone for the first time like it contains radioactive materials and their lives will be permanently altered as soon as they touch it. Other teachers have a difficult time just trying to figure out how to put it on! Instead of simply winding the string around their neck, sliding the string into slot B easily seen on the side of the microphone and turning the microphone button to the ON position, they make this task become the newest "Twenty Minute Workout" in aerobic exercise! If this task is so difficult, it makes me wonder what the rest of the year will be like.

After successfully completing this difficult chore, occasionally other situations pop up. It would be impossible to count all the times teachers have leaned over a desk drawer then slammed the drawer shut with the antenna inside, almost hanging themselves in the process!

Oh yeah! I almost forgot about my art teacher, Mrs. Cassens. One day she was cutting construction paper with a dangerous looking paper cutter that works like a guillotine. She leaned over to adjust the paper, brought the handle down, and cut the long antenna completely off the "mike" system. Wow! She was so surprised, I thought she was going to faint!

There's the dreaded "knot syndrome," too! When the teachers finally become used to the microphone, they begin to tie knots in the antenna while they teach the class. Tying knots becomes a new habit, similar to girls winding their hair around a finger while listening to the teacher or flicking the top of a pen up and down, up and down without realizing what you're doing. I've left class with the microphone antenna in so many knots it would make a Boy Scout Leader proud. Maybe I should start issuing Rope Tying Achievement badges!

I'm an easy-going kind of guy and I try to help my teachers if they feel a little awkward at first. I have a new teacher this year. He's nice, but I knew instantly he was nervous when he put the microphone on for the first time.

He walked up to me. I mean our noses were touching! He opened his mouth so wide a doctor could have used a yard stick for a tongue depressor. Very s-l-o-w-l-y, in a voice that must have been 200 decibels because it vibrated my desk across the aisle, he said, "C-a-n y-o-u h-e-a-r m-e?"

Looking at his mouth slowly opening and shutting—opening and shutting, I thought I was watching a new movie "Jaws III—Reincarnated as a Teacher!"

I sat there weighing my options. It was all I could do not to give him a pinch on the cheek and say something like, "Really, we can't go on meeting this way!" Knowing I would have to be here a whole year and remembering our recent lecture on the maturity of a sixth grader, I did the mature thing. I looked the teacher straight in the eye, which was fairly simple since his eyes were only an inch away, and mouthed very s-l-o-w-l-y, "Y-e-s I c-a-n!" even though I couldn't. He seemed happy and went back to the front of the classroom. I have a feeling it's going to be a long year in this classroom.

The best part of the auditory trainer/microphone system happens to my friend Ben. He's hard of hearing and is able to hear better with the use of this equipment. Ben has a volume control on the trainer much like turning up the sound on your television. What's great about this is, sometimes teachers forget to turn off the microphone while they have private conversations with other teachers or students. The result—you have a front row seat to everything they say! Even if they leave the room and go down the hall. You know their every move! I foresee this as having great financial possibilities. I mean, inquiring minds want to know! Unfortunately, most of the teachers catch on early but you can usually count on a slip-up now and then.

I use another piece of equipment called a closed captioner. This is a machine that hooks up to the TV and VCR set at school. When we have movies that have closed caption, whatever a person says shows up on the screen. If there's music, little musical notes appear or it says [music]. If there are loud noises, it will describe that too. This is a fantastic invention because I can keep up with popular movies and know what my friends are talking about.

Sometimes the captioner works *too well* for the teachers. We were watching a movie for a reward day last week when complete chaos broke out! During one part of the movie the main character was in a cave with what appeared to be boiling pools of thick, dark liquid all around. We were all very quiet wondering what was going to happen next when all of a sudden there were close ups of the boiling pools and the captioner started printing Burp!—fart!—burp!—fart!—burp!—fart!—all across the television screen! At first, everyone just looked at each other and then we all burst out laughing! That was the funniest part of the whole movie. Except—maybe—the teachers' faces! They were so red and their mouths were big round O's! They didn't know what to do. It was the first time I've ever seen not one, or two, but three teachers speechless! It was a moment to treasure.

Last, but certainly not least, is the "howl." I'm not talking about a timberwolf here! I'm talking about my hearing aids. They make a real high pitched sound. Of course I wouldn't know, but I've been told it's very annoying. I've had it described to me like fingernails scraping across a blackboard—but that doesn't bother me either! As a matter of fact, I kind of enjoy the weird expressions on everyone's faces when that happens. The class looks like everyone is trying to swallow mouthfuls of "tear jerkers!" I guess you could say that's another one of those "benefits" of being deaf.

The "howl" happens most of the time for me when my ear molds are loose or I lean my elbow on my desk to prop my head up. My fellow friends and classmates have become quite skilled in the art of alerting me to the problem. I can expect anything from flying objects coming at me that would make NASA jealous, a smack on the back similar to the Heimlich maneuver (almost knocking me out of my seat), to the class clutching their ears as if they were being told over the PA system they were going to receive a double helping of school lunch today.

11

Of course being a "mature" sixth grader on the "brink" of adulthood, I would never dream of making "the howl" just to aggravate some people—or would I?

That about sums up the big differences when you're mainstreamed. I know it probably sounds like a lot, but after awhile, you don't really notice these things at all. Everyone settles into a routine and suddenly I'm just like everyone else.

CHAPTER FIVE

Clothes

I've only been in school for a few weeks and I can't help but feel things are definitely different! Take for example the guys I've been going to school with since kindergarten. They used to come up with some awesome ideas to play on other kids, especially the girls! Well, now they're starting to act and look really weird.

For starters, they wear these strange pants called *zubaz* that, let me tell you, can be pretty drafty on a cold winters' day! The wind whistles through those babies like they had as many holes as a slice of Swiss cheese. And for what? To look like a zebra or another striped animal from the local zoo?

Hairstyles seem to be real important now, too. Your hair has to have all this gunk called "mousse" or "gel" smeared all over it to make it stand on end. It looks a lot like you just came out of a "hair raising" Freddy Krueger movie! One particular hairstyle I find very difficult to understand is the "lightning bolts" zig zagging through the scalp. Makes you wonder if the barber was a little shaky or had a severe nervous condition!

Another popular style seems to be the "cereal bowl" look. It looks like the barber took a bowl, set it upside down on your head and shaved off all your hair showing below the bowl. And barbers go to school for this? I could do with my cereal bowl and my dad's razor!—And a willing customer!

The girls are just as bad. They have these big bangs all "poofed" out! I'm not sure "poofed" is a word, but it sounds right.

Anyway, they have so much "gunk" on their "poofed" bangs they could run into a brick wall and they wouldn't move! I should know! I accidentally ran into one of the girls in P.E. class. Right smack into her bangs! I felt like I had been hit by a Mack truck! I thought I was going to have to be rushed to the hospital with a concussion! Instead, I was carried to the nurses office for an ice pack. The army should be informed of this secret weapon. They might be able to use it in hand-to-hand combat!

Naturally I don't want to appear "nerdish" myself so I've been trying out some of the "cool" looks. I *have* run into a few problems trying to achieve this "look."

Right now, I'm attempting to master the "pant leg thing." I keep folding the pant leg over to the side and rolling up the bottom a couple times. I still don't have the knack because I walk two feet and my pant leg unfolds again. Sometimes I use the safety pin method but I usually lose them or accidentally pin my pants to my socks! I'm not sure why this "pant thing" is so popular but I'm sure there's a reason why it's better to wear your pant legs like this (even though you have to start getting dressed a half hour earlier to achieve the "cool" look).

Wait a second! I know why! It must be to show off everyone's brand new one hundred and thirty dollar tennis shoes. Oops! Sorry! They're not *tennis* shoes anymore. They're "Pumps," "Airs," "Crosstrainers" not tennis shoes! I have to be more careful what I say. I wouldn't want to appear "uncool!"

To compliment the "cool" look ensemble, you have to have Oakleys. This was a new one to me. When everyone started talking about their "Oaks," I just figured they were talking about trees! I thought it was a strange topic of conversation for sixth graders but being deaf, sometimes I'm a step behind or I have to piece things together. I sadly discovered my discount store UV-protected sunglasses were woefully inadequate—very uncool! I also found out it would take me a year's allowance to purchase these symbolic "Oaks."

The "hottest" thing out now seems to be T-shirts that change colors, depending on different body temperatures. I admit that I fell for this fad myself—along with everyone else! I thought, "What a radical concept! Heat activated clothing! We could have hours of entertainment at school watching people turn different colors. This will be totally awesome!" At least I *thought* it would be awesome—until I had to do a report in front of the class. I suddenly found myself turning ten different colors like a brightly lit Christmas tree. No one had to ask if I was nervous. It was right there for everyone to see, in living color!

If that wasn't bad enough, I had people following me around school all day trying to touch me with their sweaty palms or breathing on my shirt trying to make me "change colors!" By the end of the day, I started wondering what these shirts were made of and begin to worry. Someone might breathe once too often on my shirt causing a "chemical reaction" disintegrating it on my body, leaving only the designer's name on my chest!

In sixth grade the "right" clothes has become a major issue. It requires hours and hours of talking, pleading, and using every trick you have to convince your parents what you need. The job is even harder if you have parents who are stuck in a "clothing time warp!" They're still in the Toughskins, flannel shirt, and Butch wax era, which may be better than the bell bottom, tie-dyed, leather jewelry, and leisure suit fad I've seen pictures of! I'm not sure? Our "styles" really aren't so different. They're *all* different! Ours are just more expensive!

CHAPTER SIX

Girls

Girls!—a small, simple, five-letter word that can cause you major headaches!

Personally, on the subject of girls, you can take 'em or leave 'em and I can leave 'em! I mean, it was fun in kindergarten or first grade when I could play tricks on girls or gross them out with worms and snakes or by taking the wings off flies I caught during class. That was the best! I thought that's why girls were put on this earth. Now I think they're here just to bug us!

I've never *really* understood girls and so I thought I would consult an authority—my dad! He said, "Jake, don't worry! You probably *never will* understand girls! I know I *still* don't understand your mom sometimes!"

This didn't sound encouraging and this "girl" thing was driving me crazy! This year seems to have gone haywire!

My friends, the "guys," have this odd look in their eyes and they're starting to act very strange around girls. Stranger than normal! They're acting as if girls are OK now! I can't believe it! The "guys" actually *want* to talk to them! What is this world coming to?

Why would they want to talk to girls anyway? They're a real pain! Especially if you have a locker next to one! When you go to get your books between classes you can barely find your locker through the haze of hair spray and perfume. Actually, I'm surprised their lockers open at all from the mountains of junk they spray. It's just like Super Glue!

I'm surprised the girls don't blind themselves from all the mirrors they have inside their lockers, next to their beauty supplies. With a little direct sunlight reflecting off all those mirrors, they could burn the school down!

I've noticed girls have found another use for their lockers this year (other than hair spray and book storage). They use their lockers for back support. For some reason, since girls have been in sixth grade, they don't seem to be able to stand up all by themselves. At the beginning of the school year it was just one or two girls, but now it has spread like wildfire!

Maybe it's some contagious disease that happens to girls at the age of twelve and thirteen. When my friends and I walk down the hallway the girls "drape"—wait! That's a curtain, isn't it? Well? I guess that's what they do! They "drape" themselves against their lockers like they don't have the energy to stand up and they watch us walk by. I don't know. Maybe vitamins would help. Or a good breakfast! After all, it *is* the most important meal of the day!

Another annoying habit the girls have started doing this year is "the giggle." They giggle all the time now! I can't hear them, but they have this smile glued to their face and their bodies shake from "the giggle." All you have to do is look at them and they start up "giggling and shaking!"

Then! They start doing this thing with their eyes. When you look at a girl or try to ask her a question, her eyelashes go up and down like a big fat, bug flew into her eye.

Last week, I thought I would be nice for a change and help Erica Stevens, a girl in my class, when she was having this "eye problem." She started with that crazy "giggle" and "eyelash" thing and said, "Oh Jake! You're *so* sweet!" Sweet! Yuk! Don't let the guys hear that!

After analyzing different theories, I think I have this "eye thing" figured out. I'm really not surprised they're having problems! This year the girls have started putting all this paint on their eyes and thick dark stuff on their lashes. It's probably hard to keep their eyes open from the weight!

Their eyes remind me of second or third grade when I would color everything in bright colors and then outline the objects with a black crayon. That's what their eyes look like!

17

The other "quirk" the girls have developed is lethal. The girls have developed a wicked right hook! The boxing world is missing a great talent in the sixth grade girls this year. For some reason I cannot explain (and it's very difficult for me to admit I can't explain something), a girl will be talking to me one minute and hit me across the hallway the next!

I've begun to feel like a human punching bag! At first I thought I must have said or done something wrong when suddenly I would find myself airborne. I was confused! Even with my *superior intellect*, I still couldn't figure out what it was. I thought I was losing my mind! No sooner would a girl slug me—the next minute she would start "the giggle!"

I was so mixed up! As a last resort I decided to get another girls' opinion—my mom's. She should know! After all, she was a girl once!

I explained the situation to my mom. I told her how desperate I was. I said, "Help me out here, Mom! I'm going to be permanently black and blue! What is their problem?"

My mom smiled and for an instant I thought *she* was going to do "the giggle!" What a nightmare! I was beginning to think I was in the Twilight Zone! I told my mom, "Smiling is not going to help me! I need some serious advice!" My mom finally told me, "Oh Jake! That just means the girl *really* likes you when she hits you. The more she hits you, the more she likes you! Really dear! It's all very simple!"

I stood there for awhile just looking at my mom, trying to make some sense of what she just told me. I felt I had just aged several years, and I was becoming an adult, carrying on a serious conversation with my parents. I just didn't know what it all meant! I thanked my mom, told her, "It made sense to me!" Then I decided my dad was right. Women! I'm never going to understand them and I'm not sure I want to!

CHAPTER SEVEN

Recess

Recess, in my opinion, is the best part of the school day. It's a time when we can show off our sixth grade status. Use our seniority. Basically, strike fear in the hearts of younger classmates! I have to admit, it feels great!

Of course, you have to follow sixth grade tradition, so your day is not complete without playing a trick on at least one lowly fourth or fifth grader.

Stealing their kick ball is top on the list of mean things to do, but just glaring at them usually sends them running! It works every time because once you're in sixth grade, you have "the power" on the playground. No one questions your authority (except for the playground supervisor who occasionally bursts our bubble of superiority).

When we finally get down to the business of playing, there's only one choice—football! Football isn't a problem for me because it's a game of secret signals and gestures I can easily understand. A high five, a slap on the back, and I know we're dazzling our opponent. The reverse is true too. I have no problem understanding when the play is broken up and everyone's face is contorted in anger. It doesn't take a genius (even though I'm right up there) to know we messed up!

Football is a good sport to show how big, strong, and tough we are now that we're in sixth grade. Playground rules only allow "touch" football but somehow we manage to get enough bumps and bruises that we have plenty to show off later to impress everyone.

I discovered that the more scrapes and bruises you have, the more popular and admired you become! Strange? I can see this is going to be another one of those things that doesn't make a lot of sense to me! I don't want to appear different so I'd better go along with it and not ask questions. To be safe, though, I better tell my mom to stock up on bandaids and ice packs. While I'm at it, maybe I should check with Dad and make sure our insurance policies are paid up!

Explaining my disheveled appearance to my mom *might* be a problem but I'm sure she'll understand when she sees the designer jeans I pleaded weeks for in shreds with blood and grass stains everywhere. Well, maybe she won't. But I know Dad will! After all, he's a "guy!"

Oh! Just in case you're wondering what the girls are doing during our display of athletic skill, they're busy doing the "drape" thing against the school building. Giggling and doing the "eyelash" thing, cheering us on! I wouldn't think that would be a lot of fun, but they seem to enjoy it and I'm learning not to question why girls do anything!

CHAPTER EIGHT

The Dance Unit

Brightly colored red, yellow, and orange leaves dancing in the wind. Early morning frosts and pumpkins decorating everyone's porch. It could only mean one thing, right!

You're probably thinking fall or maybe Halloween, but you're wrong! It means it's time once again for the annual "Dance Unit." The dreaded unit that reduces us to a mass of sweaty palms and two left feet!

Our physical education class is divided into two and three week units of different activities. Volleyball, basketball, floor hockey—fun sports! But for two *painfully* slow weeks a year, we have a dance unit that includes square dance, polka, and waltz.

Mrs. Benning, our instructor, says this is her favorite unit. Probably because she likes to see us suffer, teachers are like that! She keeps telling us how much fun it's going to be learning to dance. I'm not real sure who she's trying to convince.

To try and pump us up and spur on our enthusiasm, Mrs. Benning told us, "You will appreciate having this experience when you start going to dances at the Junior High School." Boy! The more I hear about Junior High School the less and less I want to go!

Even though I'm deaf, I have a hard time seeing my friends asking girls next year to square dance or polka to "Metallica" or "Aerosmith." I'm only familiar with CD covers, posters, and what my friends talk about, but judging from what I see, I think we're talking *major* differences between square dance and rap— polka and hard rock!

Speaking for myself, I just learn the steps so it wouldn't matter to me what music was playing.

21

When you can't hear the music, dancing can look pretty strange. I have to admit it *is* fun sometimes, watching my friends jumping around doing odd body contortions. They look like they're in a lot of pain!

You might wonder, isn't dancing difficult for a deaf person? The answer is yes and no. The most important element to learning is a good sense of humor more than a sense of rhythm!

My interpreter enjoys music so she helped me out on this unit. She brought in a stereo with two big speakers that I could put my hands or sometimes my bare feet on—as long as my feet didn't smell! Doing this, I can "feel" the song. I was surprised how well I could "feel" the difference between a fast and a slow song. Mrs. Berge and I would go through examples of different instruments. I was able to pick out songs with drums and sometimes piano and brass. While I would "feel" a song, Mrs. Berge would "become" the person in the song and sign the words, using a lot of expression. This helps me "listen" to the music and enjoy it—just like everyone else!

This method works well most of the time but square dancing can be a little more difficult. Ala man left, do si do, and promenade your lady home can be very confusing! It's even stranger watching my interpreter when she starts signing things like "duck for the oyster—dive for the clam." I start worrying if Mrs. Berge has finally gone off the deep end!

My mom always says, "If you look hard enough you will *always* learn something positive from what you're doing. Even if you don't like it!" I couldn't imagine what I could learn from this square dancing experience, but sure enough—it happened! We found all sorts of new ways to drive the girls crazy *and* have fun doing it!

When the song called for us to "swing our partner," that was our cue to twirl the girls so fast they didn't know which way they were going! "Ala man left" is a riot. We hide our hands up our sleeves and when the girls go to grab our hand, they only catch our shirt sleeve! This trick comes with a warning! If the girl gets upset, this maneuver can become dangerous. I've seen girls get so angry, they give the shirt sleeve such a huge jerk that it almost gives you a severe case of whiplash! It also makes one of your shirt sleeves two feet longer than the other one. Hence, another tough one to explain to your mom!

We only get away with our tricks the first few minutes of class because the teacher catches on fast. Boy! You would think she must have seen this happen before!

Then, she makes the worst possible threat! Mrs. Benning, in her sternest face says, "If you don't behave properly like a mature (there's that word again—mature!) sixth grader should, we will extend this unit another *two weeks* or until you get it right!"

It's amazing how our skills in dancing improved when faced with such a horrible threat!

You would think square dancing and polkas would be enough torture for any human being but then we have to do the "waltz!" Yuk! We actually have to get *close* to a girl for two or maybe three minutes at a time! This dance seems more like an endurance test! Mrs. Benning's probably waiting to see how long we can slowly move across the gym floor without killing each other! This is her payback for all the nasty things we've done to her over the years. No wonder this is her favorite unit!

Dancing this close to a girl is hard enough! *Plus* you have to concentrate on not tripping over each others' feet or marring your partner's shiny black patent leather shoes!

While all of this is going on, I look out of the corner of my eye and catch Mrs. Berge signing "Lead. Don't forget to Lead!" I thought, "Who cares! I just want to live through the next three minutes!" Talk about pressure!

I don't understand what the big deal is anyway. I can't imagine EVER wanting to waltz or get that close to a girl willingly! Mrs. Benning just smiles and winks at me as if she knows something I don't. That's impossible, of course!

CHAPTER NINE

Sign Language Class

I've been going to Lincoln Elementary School since I was "knee high to a grasshopper!" Translation—"since kindergarten." I've been wanting to say that since my grandparents explained it to me last month. Idioms can be confusing for me but I like learning about them because "hearing" people use them all the time. Not only that, they're usually pretty funny!

What was I going to talk about? Oh yes! Sign language! Several of my classmates can sign. Especially the kids I've been going to school with since Mrs. Smith's kindergarten class. Other kids only know the alphabet but it's enough to communicate. I think it's great that they try to learn!

Sometimes interpreters I've had in the past taught sign language classes during the school week. Last year my teacher allowed us to have a sign class once a week during a "free time."

We played word games, cards, bingo, and battleship. It's a lot easier to learn something when you're having fun. The teachers should try it sometime!

During sign language class, we would do things that would help my classmates understand my deafness. Sometimes I would bring in different devices that I use everyday and explain what they do and how to use them.

One time I brought in my wake-up alarm and TDD. Both machines were instant hits. Not too many people liked the idea of a vibrating pillow rudely jarring them awake in the morning. They preferred the soothing sounds of heavy metal or rap from their radio alarm clocks to start their day. My dad said given a choice, he'd take six vibrating pillows any day! This leads me to believe I'm not missing much by not experiencing a radio alarm clock.

Everyone liked my TDD. If you don't know what a TDD is, it's a device that allows me to use the telephone. It looks like a small typewriter with a place to put a telephone receiver. You can type what you want to say on the keyboard, the person you're talking with can type back his or her answer, and it will show up on a display on your TDD. Some people have paper printouts that print everything you say on paper that looks like a cash register receipt. That way you don't have to argue with a friend later when they say, "I didn't say that!" You can pull out your roll of paper and say, "Excuse me, but in paragraph six, the third sentence!" You got 'em nailed! There's only one small problem. It could be you that gets "nailed." Oh well, the TDD is a great machine and few things are perfect—but I'm working on it!

Keeping everyone interested in learning sign language can be difficult, but my interpreter seems to have found a way. When everyone becomes tired of games, she starts teaching popular songs. People bring in tapes and Mrs. Berge picks out the ones that are OK for school. It's a great way for hearing kids to learn sign language fast and my friends say it's easier for them to learn when they put the signs to music. It seems to work because almost everyone in my sixth grade can sign. It has opened up a lot of new areas for me being able to communicate so easily!

Some kids have become so skilled in sign language they thought they could use their new skill to help each other *on tests*! I don't think they realized how easy it is for an interpreter or teacher to catch on!

One day I was sitting in my science class and my teacher, Mrs. Johnson, had a test on the overhead projector. I was busily working away (like I normally am), when I noticed Mrs. Berge, my interpreter, seemed to be preoccupied watching the class. I always know something's up when she gets that "look." Of course, the steam rolling out of her collar was another good indication something was definitely amiss!

The teacher came up to talk to Mrs. Berge for a few minutes and went back to her seat. When I had finished the test, I looked at Mrs. Berge and asked, "What's up?" She said the teacher would explain when everyone was finished. Right away I thought, "Uh oh. What did I do now?" Whatever it was, I had a feeling we wouldn't be getting any "warm fuzzies" today.

When everyone finished the test, the teacher looked very unhappy. Somehow—maybe from the look on her face—I knew the word "mature" was coming. I could feel it in my bones!

Mrs. Johnson explained while she had been sitting in the back of the room, she had noticed several people using sign language during the test. Darn! And I missed it!

Mrs. Johnson continued saying, "I think it's wonderful the way so many of you are learning sign language, but there is an appropriate time and place to use it. *During a test is not one of those times!*" She went on to tell us she was very disappointed that sixth graders would do this. Mrs. Johnson said she had a list of names of the people who had been involved and she would give those people until the next day to come up to her or write a note admitting they had used sign language on the test to give answers to their friends. If they did not come forward and admit their guilt, it would mean a zero on the test!

Whoa! At least I don't have to explain this one to my mom and dad! This is one time I was completely innocent! I can feel my halo glowing! Imagine that!

Actually, it's kind of funny when you think about it. The "charge" is using sign language at an inappropriate time. I'm the *only* deaf person in the classroom and I missed it! I should have been more alert. I probably could have picked up one or two answers!

Everyone was real quiet the next day in class. I could feel the "hammer of justice" was about to come crashing down. Mrs. Johnson was about to give sentencing and we're not talking about English grammar here!

Mrs. Johnson spoke with a very serious face. She said, "I'm very pleased that the people involved in yesterday's episode came forward and admitted they had used sign language to cheat on the science test and promised to never do it again."

I thought, "What a relief!" but Mrs. Johnson looked like the worst was yet to come!

She continued saying, "Although I'm very happy those people came forward showing responsibility for their actions, I'm extremely disturbed to discover *eighteen* out of a class of *twenty-four* students admitted to using sign language on their test!"

My mind about blew a gasket! Eighteen out of twenty-four! And I missed it! I better make an appointment for an eye exam next week!

I tuned back into Mrs. Johnson's lecture to realize she had made a decision. Sign language was outlawed in science class. Anyone (with the exception of myself and Mrs. Berge) using sign language would have what they were saying "voiced" by Mrs. Berge for the whole class to hear!

Break out the scratch paper, it looks like it's back to the ancient age old custom of communication—passing notes!

Another interesting activity during our sign language time was "role playing." One role play that helped my classmates understand my deafness and become more aware of what it's like was "making" someone deaf.

We had special ear plugs and headphones someone would wear. The "deaf" person would sit at a table with a group of five or six other kids as if they were in the lunchroom.

At first, the kids didn't do much but giggle. The person who was "deaf" thought it was funny. When the people at the table realized the "deaf" person couldn't really hear them, they started laughing and telling jokes. Mostly about the new "deaf" person.

The "deaf" person became frustrated and took off the headphones and ear plugs. He looked at me and said, "How can you stand that?"

Mrs. Berge told everyone, that's why it's so important to use sign language as much as you can. At the appropriate time, of course!

There is one thing I know for certain. All the sign language classes I've had at Lincoln Elementary have helped everyone become more aware of what I go through everyday and most of my classmates try to include me in almost everything they do. Learning what you can about sign language doesn't mean you have to like me (even though I'm a real likable guy!) but it might help you understand me and maybe someone else like me.

CHAPTER TEN

Dear Santa

Christmas time! Ahhh...yes! Christmas is Santa Claus, brightly decorated Christmas trees, red and green lights, snow covered hills, sledding, skiing, shopping, presents—but best of all—Christmas is *no school for two weeks*! I'm not sure about holiday spirit but I can handle two weeks of no school!

I could almost taste the freedom of Christmas vacation when my language teacher, Mrs. Mitchell, came up with an idea. She *always* comes up with some sort of idea that usually means work! Mrs. Mitchell says we should think of her "special projects" as an opportunity to expand and explore our creative minds.

We know the moment we walk into Mrs. Mitchell's classroom, when we see her eyes sparkling and she's all bubbly and excited—we know—she's had another inspiration and we're in for another creative opportunity. Instead of visions of sugar plums dancing in our heads, we have a pulsating, brightly lit, neon sign flashing, "Run for your creative lives!"

This time, Mrs. Mitchell wants us to be Santa Claus! Excuse me! I know it's close to the holidays and there's a lot of pressure and stress this time of year. You know! Which gifts to give—entertaining—shopping (I've read about these things!) But have you lost your marbles? I suppose when Easter rolls around you'll want us to be the Easter Bunny!

Mrs. Mitchell went on to explain her inspiration. Code name—"Dear Santa." We would be partnering up with a kindergarten student and become one of Santa's "elves." Great! I suppose we have to wear red or green tights too, with shoes that have bells and curl up on the ends! The kindergartners would tell us what they wanted Santa Claus to bring them and we're supposed to ask them questions about their family and pets, if they've been good, and if they have any questions for "Santa."

Bah! Humbug! Christmas is for little kids! I'm in sixth grade now! That's kids' stuff!

Our day of "elfdom" arrived on a crisp, snowy, Christmasy kind of morning. It almost made you feel "elfish." Eerie? I was partnered with a little boy named Josh. I was a little nervous. I wasn't sure how Josh would react to my deafness but he didn't even seem to notice! He was so excited to be writing a real letter to Santa Claus, it wouldn't have mattered if I was Bigfoot himself. We were talking serious business here! Santa Claus! And you don't joke about Santa!

Josh told me about his family, all the presents he wanted, and he had a few questions he would like to ask. "Santa, how many elves do you have? Why does Rudolph's nose shine? How do reindeer fly? How do you know which house is mine? How old are you?"

Whoa! Wait a minute! I couldn't believe it! This was kind of fun. Of course I wouldn't want to admit that to Mrs. Mitchell. That could be dangerous! It could trigger *another* creative inspiration!

Too late! We received our next assignment, I mean "case"—code name "Merry Christmas!" We had to answer all of the questions the kindergartners asked in their letters, talk about their families, and wish them a Merry Christmas.

Impossible! How was I supposed to answer all of those questions when I'm still wondering about some of them myself!

Three days later, the last day of school before vacation, I was walking down the hallway when Josh came running up to me. He had just received his letter from "Santa" via the North Pole. He was so excited he was about to explode!

He jumped up and down waving the letter in the air! We didn't have to talk, it was plain to see words weren't really needed.

This Christmas Spirit thing must be for real because I was feeling like Old Saint Nick himself. Maybe there really is a Santa Claus!

I was feeling pretty good when I went back into Mrs. Mitchell's room. I looked over at Mrs. Berge. She was signing something about a book. What was that? I must have missed something. Mrs. Mitchell looked like she was going to explode from excitement. Uh-oh, this is not a good sign!

Finally I pieced it all together. We would be *writing* and *illustrating* a book when we came back from Christmas vacation. A book! Oh no!

CHAPTER ELEVEN

The Field Trip

Flowers bursting open in a rainbow of colors, trees waking with fresh, new, green leaves, flocks of birds migrating north. Oh, yes! It could only mean one thing! Lincoln Elementary School's sixth grade field trip tradition! Yet another honor to be enjoyed when achieving sixth grade status.

The whole sixth grade journeys south about seventy miles to a state park for three fun-filled days and two sleepless nights of communing with nature. We stay in cabins so we don't have to pitch a tent and sleep on the cold hard ground. We wouldn't want to go overboard with this nature stuff! A man still needs a few luxuries! I wouldn't enjoy finding myself face to face with a black bear with only a piece of canvas material between us!

There is a catch to this time honored tradition. We have to earn our way by having a sixth grade carnival with raffles of donated gifts, games, and booth activities. We're all assigned a job and hours for our contribution to our field trip. This accomplishes two things. First—cheap labor, secondly—this is once again helping us to become more *responsible* and *mature* young adults.

At this rate, I'm going to be so mature by the time I leave sixth grade I'll be able to skip middle school and move right on to high school!

The time for our trip finally arrived. Three days of nature classes at a park with all our friends! Is this heaven or what? It would be perfect if the girls weren't coming, but I'm becoming very skilled at ignoring them, so I guess it really doesn't matter.

Loading our buses with all our gear, sleeping bags, pillows, clothes, and ten pounds of snack food was a lot of work! It was all worth it when we pulled out of the school drive and saw all the younger kid's faces. They were so jealous! Sixth grade is great! Looking at the glazed eyes of the teachers and Mrs. Berge, I'm not sure they share our enthusiasm about these three days of togetherness.

We raced off the bus to explore the campground and cabins. Twenty of us were assigned to each cabin with two teachers or parents who volunteered to come along. The chaperones in our cabin were busy making sure none of us would sneak out during the night to play tricks on the girls. Not that we had even thought about doing something like that!

I still don't understand how the teachers and parents seem to *know* what we're going to do all the time. It's like they can read our minds! That's a scary thought! Sends shivers down my spine!

The first morning of Camp Smokey Bear dawned gray and drizzly. Our first class was Wilderness Survival. All right!

Walking five miles into the damp, cold woods at seven thirty in the morning with a bunch of people complaining about being "tortured" makes you wonder if the dry, warm classroom was so bad after all! Two and one half hours later, soaking wet but knowledgeable about purifying water, picking healthy berries, avoiding poisonous snakes, and finding protection from bad weather had not improved anyone's mood. Most of all—Mrs. Berge seemed to be gritting her teeth a lot!

I was having a great time and the next class was fishing! I learned a lot in this class. I didn't know there were so many varieties of worms. I didn't realize fish were such picky eaters! What didn't surprise me was the girls standing around screaming when we had to put the worms on the hooks. The guys in my group knew we wouldn't get any fishing done if we didn't help! So—we put the worms on the hooks *nice* and *slow,* so the girls would be sure to see the worms wriggle around almost as much as they were!

We thought our problems were over after we finished baiting the girls' hooks but when the teacher taught us how to cast we spent the rest of the time getting hooks out of trees, bushes, and almost anything on land! Girls!

The fishing was looking hopeless for us guys until the teacher pulled out his secret weapon. His sure fire "fish catcher!" Guaranteed to catch a big one! Everyone gathered close wondering what it could be? Then he held it up. With a big smile on his face he said, "Leeches!" The girls went screaming off in the direction of the lodge creating a cloud of dust the state of Kansas would be proud of. You would have thought the instructor had announced all cans of hair mousse were being confiscated from the girls' cabins!

The day went so fast I couldn't believe it! Here it was. Six P.M. already! We had been going non-stop for almost ten hours! It didn't seem that long at all! I turned and saw Mrs. Berge, mud splattered, hair blown in all directions, and dark circles under her eyes. I walked up to her and said, "Isn't this the most fun you've ever had? I can't wait until tomorrow! We have bird watching, compass class, and the traditional ten mile hike ending with a huge bonfire! This is fantastic!" Strange. I thought she would have looked more excited!

After supper we had a *special* surprise. A park ranger came and brought some animals, that are found in the area, to talk about. I was jealous of Mrs. Berge because she stood up front next to the ranger. She could see all the animals close up! We weren't sure what all the animals were because they were covered up.

The ranger showed us two different owls. They were awesome! Their necks looked like they could turn completely around! When the ranger finished talking about the different kinds of owls, he took the cover off the next group of boxes.

My eyes almost popped out of my head! Snakes! Cool! I looked over at Mrs. Berge to tell her how lucky she was to see everything so close up when I noticed she looked real peculiar! Her face was completely white, like she had seen a ghost and her eyes were as big as koosh balls!

The ranger kept talking about the different snakes. She even brought a rattlesnake! The ranger was almost finished talking about snakes when she decided to take one of the harmless ones out of the box and hold it while she talked. I couldn't believe this ranger was a girl and she liked snakes! She was something special. You don't find girls like her everyday!

Mrs. Berge was trying real hard to ignore the snake beside her when all of sudden the snake's head came up and stuck it's forked tongue out towards her. Everyone laughed but I thought Mrs. Berge was going to faint! I'm getting a strong feeling she doesn't like snakes!

The ranger finished her demonstration and told us there was one more program set up outside. It was dusk, and we all gathered around the other ranger. He had brought hawks and other birds that they had helped recover from injuries.

The fresh air seemed to have revived Mrs. Berge. She looked a lot better!

The ranger talked about each bird when suddenly he told us, "In a moment you will see something fly by, so keep your eyes open!" We were all excited! In a flash something flew past Mrs. Berge. At first she brushed it away like a mosquito or a moth. Then, three or four more flew by until we all realized what they were! Bats! This place is totally cool! Mrs. Berge is so lucky! First snakes and now bats! What more could a guy ask for!

It was a dynamite three days for me but I'm not sure Mrs. Berge will ever talk to me again! I guess I really can't blame her. Can you imagine anything worse than staying in a small cabin with twenty girls doing the "giggle" and using so much hair spray they've probably doubled the size of the hole in the ozone layer! It's no wonder she looks shot! I can't imagine what else it could be. Personally, I'm ready to go again next week!

CHAPTER TWELVE

Tribute To Mr. McCarthy

Teachers come in a variety of shapes, sizes, and personalities. Some are men and some are women. They can be tall or short—skinny as a flagpole or as plump as a prize winning pumpkin. They're all different! No two are alike. Naturally the most important characteristic of all, is whether they're *mean* or *nice*!

Each year you're given a new teacher you have to analyze and evaluate. You have to nurture and mold this person to your specifications of the perfect teacher. Proper training is critical and sometimes very tricky. You have to remember, teachers can be the key to having a year that flies by or one that seems like it's forever!

After attending only one day of school, my instincts told me Mr. McCarthy, my homeroom teacher, was going to be my biggest challenge yet!

I had heard stories from students who had had Mr. McCarthy in the past, but I wasn't worried. Mr. McCarthy might take a little longer to perfect, but I had confidence. One week, maybe two, he'd be "eating out of my hand!" I've logged a lot of hours analyzing teachers. Learning what makes them "tick." It requires expertise in two areas. A keen mind and logical thinking. I possess both, of course!

There is a reason for going to all this trouble. You have to discover their vulnerable areas. It's crucial! Knowing this valuable bit of information, you'll be able to pinpoint exactly what you can get away with!

I have to admit, there has been an occasion or two that I've allowed my deafness to play on my teachers sympathies. Especially when I was in trouble! Naturally, this seldom happened but it's reassuring to know there is a "fool proof" ploy to fall back on.

Yes siree—this year's going to be a "piece of cake!" A real breeze!

A FEW FRUSTRATING MONTHS LATER

We're halfway through the school year and I have to confess! Mr. McCarthy is still a puzzle to me. He's different from any teacher I've had before!

He has a sense of humor that keeps you guessing all the time. One minute Mr. McCarthy looks at you with his eyes shooting sparks and his eyebrows become one continuous dark line across his forehead forming a scowl, aimed directly at you! His nostrils flare and you expect to see smoke puffing out of them like a bull charging a red cape! You don't know whether to yell "olé'" or "run for your life!" Your whole body starts breaking out in a sweat. There's so much water coming out of your pores, you feel like a human sprinkler system! Just when you think you should start making funeral arrangements, Mr. McCarthy smiles and tells a joke or says something funny.

Of course you're not laughing because your whole body is still in shock! It takes a few minutes before your blood starts pumping, sending messages to your brain telling you it's OK to breathe again! I'd better check our community education schedule for CPR classes. I have a feeling this may be a useful skill to have this year.

Mr. McCarthy expects certain behavior from all of his students. If not, you'll find yourself in the hallway faster than a blink of an eye.

A crook of his finger motioning to the front door strikes fear in the hearts of the whole sixth grade and brings instantaneous panic to the classroom! Wondering who's next? Who will disappear into the hallway? The hallway has always been a place for teachers to discipline students, but this year the hallway has become known as the "Hall of Doom!"

When Mr. McCarthy summons you to the hallway, you know you're in deep trouble! Not just your name on the board or a reprimand. I'm talking hard-time! No recess! Worse yet, eating your lunch with Mr. McCarthy! Talk about torture! Eating your lunch with your teacher!

I remember the time three people went into the "Hall of Doom" and only Mr. McCarthy returned! He's killed them! We just knew it! Everyone was afraid to ask the question we were all dying to know! Where were they? We all sat motionless. No one even breathed. Mr. McCarthy just stood in front of the class, looking at us with his serious look and familiar scowl. In a deep voice he said, "I ate 'em!" Twenty-six mouths dropped open in shock! No one dared to say a thing!

I was busy "patting myself on the back" for successfully avoiding a personal journey to the "Hall of Doom" when a dark cloud seemed to settle over my desk. I knew my day of reckoning had come.

It all happened so fast! I had just come back from a rousing game of football with the guys. We were still pushing each other around and having some fun. I sat down at my desk. I decided it would be hilarious to put my feet under Jimmy Dixon's chair in front of me and move it just a little when he sat down. How was I to know he'd fall flat on the floor and look like an octopus with eight arms and legs going in every direction! If THIS wasn't bad enough, he knocked two desks over on his way down! Books, pens, and paper went everywhere!

One look at Mr. McCarthy's face confirmed my worst fear. My time had definitely come to disappear into the "Hall of Doom!"

My mind raced furiously with all the data I had collected over the years. I was quickly deciding on my options. Only the best excuse was going to work!

I slowly dragged my feet across the floor, my shoulders hunched in defeat, trying to delay what was to come. Unfortunately, I had worn my body temperature controlled T-shirt and I was changing colors as fast as the neon scoreboard at the ballpark when you hit a homerun!

I went out into the hallway and I stood in a pool of sweat, dripping from my body. Waiting! I'm surprised my shirt didn't short circuit from all the moisture!

My one and only hope of Mr. McCarthy being intimidated by my deafness dissolved before my very eyes. He stood nose to nose with me! My interpreter did not exist. Mr. McCarthy didn't look at anyone but me! A prayer and a promise to attend Sunday school and church every Sunday for the rest of my life seemed like a real good idea about now!

Mr. McCArthy asked *one* question. "Why?"

My first reply was, "I don't know." It was the first thing that came to my mind and it just popped out.

Immediately I could see by the veins pulsating at his temples, that was not the answer he was looking for!

There comes a time in your life when you realize you're responsible for your own behavior. I had a feeling my time was now! I also knew there hadn't been a story invented creative enough to get me out of this situation. The only thing left was to tell the truth and accept the consequences that were sure to follow.

I heard that confession is good for the soul! By the time I had finished talking, I had confessed to everything! Every prank I had done since kindergarten! I even told Mr. McCarthy about the time I hid Mrs. Smith's "Mr. Happy" smiley face she used everyday. I was so proud of myself for pulling off the best trick of the year! My feeling of pride didn't last long. I can still remember Mrs. Smith saying, "I feel bad that 'Mr. Happy' is missing but I'll just take 'Mr.

Sad' and turn his frown upside down! See how easy it is to become 'Mr. Happy'!"

Wait a minute! Someone stop me! I can't seem to stop babbling! I looked at Mrs. Berge, and she just continued voicing everything I was signing.

I finally got myself under control again. I looked up and I was shocked to see admiration on Mr. McCarthy's face. He patted me on the back, shook my hand, and said, "Don't you feel better for telling the truth and not trying to lie your way through an explanation!"

I stood for a moment and to my surprise, it *did* feel good. I felt like a huge weight had been lifted off my shoulders. Of course, this didn't mean I wasn't going to be punished but I had a new respect for Mr. McCarthy. He's an "OK" guy!

I didn't want to have these "chats" often but I knew then if ever I had a problem I could talk it over with Mr. McCarthy, man to man!

Every year we have several different teachers to work with and some make bigger impressions on us than others. This year may not be over with yet, but I already know Mr. McCarthy's a special kind of guy and I know I'm going to remember him until I'm a very old man. *At least forty or so!*

CHAPTER THIRTEEN

Showtime
LIGHTS! CAMERAS! ACTION!

Every year our class has a music program. Each grade level has one during the year. I have to admit, this is about the only time of the year I don't feel a part of the class.

Music is OK, but singing—ugh! The last couple of years I've decided to attend speech class during our music time. Speech class is hard enough learning how to correctly pronounce words, but singing! It's a nightmare!

I can have music class interpreted but I'm always two or three words behind everyone else so I always end up singing solo. My voice isn't one that would sell millions of records and I haven't been saving any space on my bedroom wall for gold and platinum albums!

Mrs. Berge could see my frustration so she talked to me about it. She had directed a sign language program before and she asked me if I would be interested in doing something like that with the class. I thought it was a fantastic idea! It was something I could really be involved in.

Mr. McCarthy gave Mrs. Berge permission to talk the idea over with the rest of the sixth grade to see how they felt about it. We held a meeting in our commons area and watched a video-tape of the program Mrs. Berge had directed to give everyone an idea of what was involved. Study time and recess would be the only time we could have to practice and only if our schoolwork was finished.

Everyone seemed excited about doing something different; but I was flabbergasted! (Isn't that a great word, I love to try out new words!) Anyway, I was flabbergasted when I found out that sixty-eight people had signed up out of a class of eighty-six!

My reaction was nothing compared to the state of shock Mrs. Berge seemed to be in! She started mumbling. Kind of like my mom does now-a-days! It looked like she was saying, "Sixty-eight! Sixty-eight!" Over and over again! You would think she didn't enjoy being with all of us. How lucky can she get! All sixty-eight of us at one time! Sounds like fun to me!

When Mrs. Berge recovered from her initial shock, we had our first meeting. Everyone had ideas! We decided on "At The Movies" for the theme to our program. Mrs. Berge warned us that we had to pick something appropriate for school and she, of course, had final say! It didn't really matter to me, it just sounded like a lot of fun!

Mrs. Berge decided on seven different theme songs from movies we had suggested and one or two of her own. She chose different people for each song and set up a cast for each theme song.

I think Mrs. Berge was a little frazzled because of all the people who had signed up. She gave us a *long* lecture about responsibility and maturity. I think she's been interpreting too many lectures about this subject! She was starting to sound just like the teachers! Mrs. Berge told us we had better show up for our scheduled practice times. We had three chances! If we didn't show up the fourth time, we were out! Unless, we had a real good excuse—*signed in blood*! She told us it would be our responsibility to check the sign language informational board in each classroom for practice times, AND BE THERE!

Boy! She seemed a teensy bit grumpy! How much work could it be anyway? She was only giving up half her lunch period and her free study time, five days a week for the next three months! I mean, look at us. We were giving up *football* once or twice a week! It was no big sacrifice for the girls. They didn't do anything anyway! But no football! That was asking a lot!

Mrs. Berge and I started practicing together first. I had to memorize the words to the song Mrs. Berge had picked out for me. Then, I had to take time to "feel" the song like I had during the square dance unit. Mrs. Berge went through the song several times, expressively acting out the song so I would understand it better.

She met with each one of the lead signers of the songs to practice, much like you would rehearse with a lead singer. Often I would just sit and watch.

It was a very slow process. First, the person had to listen to and memorize the song normally, then learn the signs. Finally, the singer had to add expression. Mrs. Berge jumped up and down and was *always* signing, "I want more expression! You have to become the person in the song!"

I thought it was going well but some people were getting a strange look in their eyes. I feared mutiny or a lynch mob soon!

When the lead signers were starting to feel comfortable, Mrs. Berge began practicing with the chorus. Most of the songs Mrs. Berge chose had large choral groups. She wanted everyone who had signed up to have a part. Some of the people were chosen to mime playing musical instruments that were in the song, because Mrs. Berge wanted each song to be acted out exactly like a play.

I was certain several of my classmates would become bored and drop out but almost everyone stuck with it. I was surprised! More and more people were starting to sign to me too! Signing was becoming comfortable and natural for them.

When the lead signers and their chorus were practicing together, it was time to work with the two narrators. They had the toughest job! They had to memorize a whole script and learn all the signs because the whole program was in sign language.

The story was set on the two narrators coming upon a deserted old movie theater. They decided to go in and explore. Finding a stack of old video tapes and a machine that still worked, the two girls talked about the video tapes and slipped each one into the machine. They sat back and watched the videos appear on the screen. We had made huge backdrops for each movie the narrators would play in the machine. When the girls sat back to watch the movies, that was our cue to become the theme song.

It was a *tremendous* amount of work and there were days when we were sure it was never going to come together!

After hours and hours of practice, making props, and screen backdrops, our day of stardom had arrived.

Everyone was a nervous wreck! Especially me! I had a squadron of butterflies flying reconnaissance missions in my stomach! My mom tried to make me feel better at breakfast. She told me, "Now Jake, just imagine the whole audience sitting there *in their underwear*!"

My jaw almost hit the floor! I couldn't believe *my* mother would say something like that! It *was* funny to picture a few of the teachers in their underwear but I couldn't help wondering about my mom's mental condition! What's gotten in to her this year!

IT'S SHOWTIME!

All of our rehearsing was over. I stood on the risers looking out at a packed gymnasium *full of video cameras*! The butterflies in my stomach set out on another sortie. I just hoped I wouldn't faint! How embarrassing! Why does the word "underwear" keep popping up in my mind?

The "Old City Theater" was ready! Narrators were exploring. There was no turning back now!

The first movie was put into place. It was "Nine To Five." None of us was too familiar with this movie but it was always our favorite one to practice. All the girls were

46

dressed up as secretaries and Mr. McCarthy played the mean boss. He was dressed up like a real nerd! It was hilarious! He had on a plaid sport coat with checkered pants. He wore the strangest tie I've ever seen and half of his shirt tail was hanging out. The best part was his hair and his glasses! His hair looked like it had been caught in a wind tunnel and his glasses were so big and ugly they would have stopped a freight train!

When Mr. McCarthy walked out on his cue the audience went wild! He was an instant star!

At the end of the song, the girls tied up Mr. McCarthy and rolled him out of the gym on his chair. They were having a terrific time tying Mr. McCarthy in knots. I sure hoped he trusted those girls to let him loose later!

When the crowd had settled down, we went into our next movie, "Ghostbusters." This was a BIG set. The girls were all dressed in white with Ghostbuster T-shirts. They were waving ghosts and hiding behind crates and boxes. The guys were dressed all in black, searching for the "ghosts." There were flashing red police lights and props everywhere! It was a fun song to watch and the audience seemed to enjoy it, especially the little kids!

The next movie was all Mrs. Berge's idea. She thought it would be fun to add a touch of class to our program so she picked out one of her favorites. It was called "Tonight" from a movie called "West Side Story."

I was real happy she didn't pick me for this song. It was a *romantic* song. Yuck! That would be pure torture! There weren't any flashing lights, neat props, or fun instruments. Just two ladders. That's all. I looked at the audience. I was sure this one was going to be a flop.

Jeff Taylor, the unlucky soul Mrs. Berge chose to play the character from the movie, is one of the best signers around. The girls think he's the coolest! They practically drool all over him! You know what's *really* strange about all of this, Jeff seems to actually enjoy it! Maybe because

47

Mindy Benson (the girl character in the song) is OK. For a girl—I mean. I guess you could say she's kind of cute. At least Jeff sure seems to think so. When they finished their song, heads snuggled together, walking hand in hand off the stage, I was surprised to see that the audience really seemed to enjoy it! They had an odd look on their faces and their eyes looked like they were going to cry or something. I probably would have looked teary eyed too if I were Jeff and had to put my head together with Mindy Benson and walk hand in hand off the set looking all mushy—ugh!

We picked up the tempo with the next theme song from the movie "Flashdance." The girls were all dressed up in aerobic outfits and leg warmers. It started out slow but they began exercising, dancing, and signing while they jumped around all over the gym. Their timing looked neat! They were all dancing and signing together. It looked great but I couldn't really enjoy it completely. I was nervously awaiting my big moment. I was next!

I was doing "Somewhere Out There" from the movie "An American Tale." It was just me and Karen Jenkins, a girl I have grown up with. Yep. Just the two of us. In the middle of the gym floor with the *whole school* watching us!

I was dressed up like a mouse wearing a red tunic and a huge blue hat with enormous ears, a mouse nose stuck to mine, and a huge gray tail trailing behind me! *Why should I feel strange?* Another one of Mrs. Berge's ideas! I can still see her saying, "Become the character in the song!"

At least I wasn't alone! My friend Karen was dressed up as a mouse too! She had on a hoop skirt, a big blouse, and a scarf for a hat with ears that matched mine. She even had the nose and tail! We were really in this together!

I saw our backdrop set into place. It was time! Mrs. Berge was sitting on the gym floor giving me my cues. My knees were knocking so badly I wasn't sure I could walk! At that moment, I didn't think I was missing much by not doing music programs with the rest of the class if this was what it was like.

I looked at the little kids long enough to see they were excited and having a good time. Their mouths were shaped like little cheerios oohing and aahing! I began to think, "Maybe this isn't so bad after all!"

When our song was finished, Mrs. Berge had us walk hand in hand off stage. We were supposed to act happy because in the movie we had just found each other. This acting stuff is tough! It was OK because it was Karen but even that was bad enough! Karen and I are much more comfortable *arguing* with each other!

The backdrop changed and everyone's face lit up like a light bulb! A huge group of people came out on stage to do "The Little Mermaid."

Mrs. Berge had been worried about this song because our "lead fish" broke his "fin"—oops! —I mean arm! We didn't have understudies and there wasn't enough time to train another "fish"—person! Oh well, we put a red crab shell on him and you hardly even noticed he was only using one "claw"—Sorry! Hand!

Andrea Sanders, the girl who played the little mermaid, seemed to be an instant hit with all the boys from kindergarten to fifth grade. I could almost see the hearts coming out of their eyes. They had dazed expressions on their faces like they'd just been hit over the head with a baseball bat. They really looked silly. That's *never* gonna happen to me!

We made it! We were all ready to go into our final song "Come To America" when Mrs. Berge surprised us by dedicating a song to us.

She told us how proud she was of each and every one of us for not only our eagerness to try something new but to also accept the responsibility involved in putting a program together. Most important of all, she wanted to thank us for our willingness to give up our football time! She winked when she said that and several people laughed—I could see them!

Gee! And I thought all this time Mrs. Berge didn't understand what she was asking us to give up!

Mrs. Berge continued thanking us for our support. She turned to us and said, "You truly are the 'wind beneath my wings,' so I would like to do that song—just for you."

We sat down and were surprised when all the lights suddenly went out. The gym was pitch black!

Immediately I thought, "What a time for a power outage. Mrs. Berge is gonna have a cow!"

Then I looked up and saw two beautiful white hands. Nothing else. Hands—glowing in the dark, moving very expressively in sign language. Mrs. Berge was signing the song, "Wind Beneath My Wings" using a black light. It was totally cool!

When she finished, the lights went back on. Everyone was completely still for a moment and then they all started clapping excitedly. We were stomping our feet on the risers and clapping. We loved it!

People were STILL clapping when we started the strobe light and drummers and flag people took their positions. We were ready to perform the "Grand Finale." All of the cast came together to sign as one big group—even Mr. McCarthy! No one wanted to stand too close to him though, because when he signed the word "far," you had to duck or risk getting slugged! I just thought it was super that he wanted to try. Actually, I was proud of everyone. I don't know when I've enjoyed myself more. I didn't want it to end!

Maybe I should talk with Mrs. Berge after the program about doing this again next year. Yeah! That would be great!

I looked over at Mrs. Berge. She looked wiped out! Relieved, but definitely wiped out! Kind of like she looked on our way back from our three day "back to nature" field trip. Maybe I'd better wait until Monday!

CHAPTER FOURTEEN

Our Turn

The trees had all blossomed, the flowers were blooming, and the days were getting warmer. May was here. My favorite time of the year!

Like at the Kennedy Space Center, the countdown had begun. Yes! Our sixth grade year was almost a memory!

The warm spring sun was shining brightly through the classroom window. I could sense the lakes and woods calling me. I could feel the cool water splashing my face as I ran head long into the lake and the heat of the sun-warmed grass as I lay on my back with my fishing rod baited and ready at my side.

Suddenly my summertime dream was burst by my social studies teacher, Mr. McCarthy, reminding the class that, "School isn't over yet and even though it's difficult, we still have work to do!"

Darn! They sure knew how to spoil a perfectly good dream. I don't think teachers understand what they're asking of us. They're just teachers! They don't know what it's like to be a kid and be stuck in school when there are so many things you'd rather be doing. Important things! Having fun! What would *they* know! They *like* school!

I turned and noticed Mrs. Berge had stopped signing. Uh oh! I knew instantly, when her hands stopped moving, she was aware I was not paying attention. I'd been caught! Trapped like a rat!

Sometimes Mrs. Berge would sign things completely different from what the teacher was saying because she knew she'd caught me not listening, AGAIN!

One day in health class, where I tended to daydream often, I looked up and I was positive Mrs. Berge was signing "The

Twelve Days Of Christmas!" I spent the next five minutes trying to figure out what a partridge in a pear tree had to do with a cell membrane!

I "tuned" back in to Mr. McCarthy's lecture to find out he was giving us an assignment he thought we would enjoy. I was immediately skeptical. In my vast academic career, the last assignment I enjoyed was in kindergarten class. Finger-painting! I finger-painted the picture, the table, my clothes, and a few friends!

Forcing myself to pay attention, Mr. McCarthy continued explaining our assignment. He said, "*You* will be teaching social studies class." Whoa! Back up there! Could you say that again? I could have sworn Mr. McCarthy said *we* would be teaching class!

"That's right," Mr. McCarthy said. "You and a partner will do the outlining of a chapter, present it to the class, and be responsible for control of classroom behavior. You may use my teacher's manual, film strips, whatever you need to present your chapter. Of course, you will be graded on your presentation."

Yes! What an easy assignment! Piece of cake! What a fantastic way to finish the school year! *Students* teaching class! We had got it made!

Just a few days later I was talking to myself. "Jake! Jake! Jake! When will you ever learn!"

It was true! Spring fever must have momentarily caught me off guard. I should have known there was some sort of lesson to be gained from this experience. I just couldn't imagine how this assignment could be anything but a lot of fun!

We would be the teachers. What was so difficult about that? The only difficult part I could think of was getting up in front of the whole class, but I was as comfortable with that as anyone else. I would do all the work and Mrs. Berge would "voice" for me. Everyone was used to my

53

presentations by then, so that wouldn't be a problem. Besides! *We* would be in control! What could possibly go wrong?

Wrong? I should have said, "What could possibly go right?" Everything went haywire!

My frustration started while outlining the chapter notes, making overhead transparencies for class, planning activities, trying to fill a *fifty* minute class time. This was a lot more work than I thought it would be. Homework would have been faster and easier!

Things steadily became worse. When the time came for us to start teaching our chapters, I hadn't counted on my classmates becoming power hungry dictators!

Everyday two people went to the front of the classroom. Their egos inflated ten times for each step closer they came to the front of the room. The power went straight to their heads!

I had thought foolishly that everyone would make the hour as easy as possible. Games. Filmstrips. Maybe a few notes. It was the complete opposite. Each day the "dynamic duo" in front of the class made each chapter as difficult as they possibly could. It was becoming a contest! Who could make their chapter the hardest!

I couldn't believe it. My chapter outline was changing daily. Just wait!

The day of "dictatorship" for my partner, Sue Thomas, and myself had come. Payback time!

I stood up in front of the classroom. Instantly I became aware that things looked a lot different looking out over the classroom when responsibility for the whole hour rested on *our* shoulders! The class looked at us for about a second and then they continued talking and not paying attention to us.

I thought, "How rude! They know there's someone up here trying to speak!"

When Sue and I presented the chapter with notes on the overhead, the whole class started to make faces and complain. Fortunately for me, I couldn't hear it but it was easy to see the distress on their faces. Boy! You would think we were asking them to turn in a ten page report on the Roman Empire by tomorrow! Get a grip here people!

Next, Sue gave instructions for a ten point quiz. She slowly and carefully gave the class step-by-step directions. Sue repeated *several times*, they could *not* use their books.

Stacy Cunningham (notorious for not paying attention) raised her hand. Sue answered, "Yes. Do you have a question Stacy?" Stacy asked, "Can we use our books?" Sue calmly repeated, "No, you may not."

We were almost ready to start the quiz when two more people raised their hands. Sue called on them. "Can we use our books?"

I couldn't believe it! What was their problem? I'm the one who's deaf!

When we thought everyone had *finally* grasped the concept, *they could not use their books,* we figured that our problems would be over.

Wrong. One person came up to us, "Can I get a drink?" We didn't want to appear heartless so we said, "OK." A minute later another person came up, "Can I go to the bathroom?" Then it was like a game of dominos, one person after another with a hundred excuses! "I forgot my notebook in my locker!" "Can I sharpen my pencil?"

Wait a minute! This was getting out of control! I couldn't help myself. I said, "Can't you be more organized! You're in *sixth* grade now! Not *first*! You should be able to accept some responsibility by now! What's going to happen next year when you're in junior high school? Who's going to hold your hand?" Mrs. Berge was furiously voicing for me.

Something "clicked" in my brain and I realized I was acting exactly like the teachers. Oh no! If nothing else, I had the class' complete attention. They just stared at me as if I had lost my mind.

I looked up to see Mr. McCarthy with a big grin on his face. He *knew* this was going to happen. I couldn't believe it. All of us for the last two weeks were guilty of sounding just like a teacher!

Surely *we* didn't give Mr. McCarthy as hard a time as this group gave *us*! Did we? What a chilling thought!

This role reversal thing was pretty scary. It should have come with a warning label! I can't speak for Sue but I think I preferred being a student for a while longer. I hoped there weren't any more "enjoyable" assignments before graduation. I might not survive the fun!

CHAPTER FIFTEEN

Graduation Day

I awoke to the vibrating motion from my alarm as usual. I thought, "Just another school day." Then, I remembered! It was not just another school day! It was the last day of school! Graduation Day!

I jumped out of bed, surprised how much energy I had. Normally my mom has to come in three times and then drag me out of bed. Sometimes she threatens me with a bucket of water but I think she would *really* do it!

I looked out my window to see the sun shining. It was going to be a wonderful day. My last day at Lincoln Elementary School! Never again would I have to walk those hallways! I was NEVER going to miss that place! Once I left, I was NEVER stepping foot in that school again!

I'd better get dressed, I thought I wouldn't want to be late for the last day! I reached over to one of my "piles" of clothes which I usually had lying around, to put something on, when I spied some clothes hanging on my door.

Oh yeah! I forgot. Mom and Dad said I had to wear my good clothes. I don't know why. No one else would be all dressed up. I was going to stick out like a real nerd! I guessed it could be worse. They could have make me wear a suit! I was lucky. Dad stuck up for me and said he really didn't think I needed to wear one. Probably because Dad felt the same way I do about suits. If it's not a funeral, wedding, or church—*you don't need to wear one*!

I remember last year when Mom told Dad he had to buy a new suit. You would have thought Mom told him the dentist was going to pull out all his teeth! No one could talk to Dad for a week! And when the final purchase was made, Mom vowed she was never going shopping with Dad again!

I dressed and combed my hair, making sure I had just enough height on my "side spike" and mousse and gel to make it stay. I wouldn't want it to go flat today! I even splashed on a little "Old Spice." Why not!

I went out into the living room to find Dad loading up the video camera. "Dad! You're not going to take *that*, are you?" I had a flashback of that first day of school when I had dodged all those parents in the hallway taking videos of "The First Day Of School!"

My dad put his arm around me and said, "You'll be glad we did this, someday!" I seriously doubted that!

Riding along in the car, I thought to myself, "It's almost like I've come full circle. Mom and Dad took me to that special FIRST day of school when I was a kindergartner to make sure everything went OK. Now, here I am. My parents are taking me for another special day. The very LAST day of elementary school! Eerie!"

Mom and Dad went racing to the gym to get prime video space and I went to my classroom. There weren't any little "shrimps," kindergartners, to get in my way. They had finished school yesterday. I walked by the first, second, and third graders. They were busy in the commons area getting ready for a movie and treats to celebrate the last day of school.

I was continuing my final journey through the hallway and I noticed the fourth graders lining up for their annual walk to the city park and the fifth graders getting ready for a final kick ball tournament and ice cream party. I *knew* what they were doing. I had already experienced each grade's traditional "last day of school activity." It seemed like it was a hundred years ago!

I made that final bend in the hallway that would lead me to—the sixth grade hallway!

Strange! I wasn't feeling so sure of myself like I had at the beginning of the year!

There was an unusual calmness. No one was running around, getting books, spraying perfume. It was calm.

I walked into the classroom and couldn't believe my eyes! The "guys" were dressed like I've never seen them before—like me! Obviously they had a similar discussion with their parents on proper attire for graduation. It was also clear, they were as uncomfortable as I was!

The girls looked different too! What was it? Their bangs were still "poofed" and combat ready. They still had the "eyelash" problem and body shaking "giggle" but—there was something different.

Dresses! They're all wearing dresses! I was so used to Spandex, blue jeans, and stretch pants—it was a surprise to actually see they had legs! Kneecaps even!

They looked...nice! I can't believe I said that! Something weird is happening again.

Mr. McCarthy was dressed in his finest suit and tie. In a couple of hours the "Hall of Doom" would only be a memory. A very vivid memory!

It was hard to believe my elementary school years were almost over. It was time to line up. We had practiced yesterday and everyone was laughing and pushing each other around. Some people even walked funny on purpose to upset the teachers!

This day was different. Everyone was nervously lining up. Suddenly it felt like there were a *million* butterflies in my stomach.

Finally, it was my turn. I entered the gym. I carefully paced my steps like I had in rehearsal yesterday. I looked up. The gym had never looked so nice!

All the way around the gym, Mrs. Mitchell had put up our silhouettes that she had made recently in art class. The whole graduating class surrounded us.

There were green plants everywhere! The teachers must have gone around and gathered up every plant in the whole school!

A huge brightly colored banner congratulating the graduating class hung on another wall. In the middle of all these decorations were eighty-six chairs. Our place of honor for the next hour and a half.

Mr. McCarthy, Mrs. Mitchell, and Mr. Wescott gave special awards for social studies, science and English. Then, Mrs. Benning gave out physical fitness awards. I still think all of us should receive awards for surviving the dance unit! The principal stood and congratulated our class on a successful year and complimented us on our excellent representation of the sixth grade.

When the special awards had been given out and all the speeches made, it was time for the diplomas.

One by one our names were read and we walked up to accept our diploma and shake hands with Mr. McCarthy. When the last diploma was handed out I could feel the sigh of relief from my classmates. The hardest part was over!

Now it was time for the class song. Each year the sixth grade class picked out a song to do for their parents. We had chosen "Come To America." Everyone thought that was the perfect song to do. We had performed "Come To America" for our finale to our sign language program and the class decided it would be nice to be able to sign our graduation song. It made me feel good inside that the kids were so comfortable signing. It made me feel more a part of the class!

When it was time for our "recessional" march, we were feeling a lot more relaxed! Our step was faster and more self-assured. Once we cleared the gym doors we whooped it up and patted each other on the back. We'd done it. We *finally* made it!

The celebrating continued for about fifteen minutes before it finally sunk in. We could leave! We could just walk out those doors of Lincoln Elementary School and never come back!

I paused for a moment to think about this last year. I decided I *should* probably say good-bye to Mr. McCarthy. After all, he was my homeroom teacher. It wouldn't take up too much of my time. It would probably make him feel good, too! Teachers are like that.

I went back to my old room and found out most of the class had the same idea! I didn't understand. Everyone seemed reluctant to leave! What was even stranger, I felt like I was leaving home. Sure, we have disagreements with classmates and teachers, but it's *home*. And it's *safe*.

Next year would be completely different. Junior high school! It would be all new. A lot more kids. Older kids. We would be *sevys*. The dreaded *sevys*.

I was starting to hyperventilate when Mr. McCarthy came up to me. He must have noticed I was having a nervous break- down! Much like the day we "chatted" in the hallway!

We shook hands, and he congratulated me on graduating. He told me he, too, had learned a lot this year by having me in his classroom and wanted to thank me for it. I was starting to relax. Mr. McCarthy was making me feel more confident already. He said, "Knowing how much you like sports, I suppose you'll be signing up for football, skiing, track, or basketball next year."

I brightened for a second. I hadn't even thought about that. I was so worried about becoming a *sevy*, I never even thought about all the extra activities I could do that I couldn't in elementary school.

Suddenly, it didn't feel so awful. I turned to Mrs. Berge and said, "Football! I've *always* wanted to try out for football and I love to ski! Doesn't that sound great! You are going to interpret for me next year, aren't you? "Yes sir! I can just feel the crisp autumn air, the cracking of football helmets, cold powdery slopes in the winter. It should be fun! Don't you think so? I can't wait!"

I turned to Mr. McCarthy as Mrs. Berge voiced for me, "Thanks a lot Mr. McCarthy. Maybe I'll drop by next year and tell ya how things are going. It won't be any problem. I could stop by and say, 'Hi!' to Mrs. Mitchell and Mr. Wescott, too. I might even pop in and say, 'Hi!' to some of my other teachers. I don't mind at all. I'll just be across the parking lot next year. Not far at all! When football starts, I'll let you know my game schedule. Maybe you'll want to stop by—."